All I Have in This World

Also by Michael Parker

Hello Down There
The Geographical Cure
Towns Without Rivers
Virginia Lovers
If You Want Me to Stay
Don't Make Me Stop Now
The Watery Part of the World